AF

**When Mr. Potts, the principal,
looked out of his window
and saw the school buses spinning,**

he knew it was going to be a ...

BAD DAY AT MONSTER ELEMENTARY

By MIKE THALER • pictures by JARED LEE

AN AVON CAMELOT BOOK

For Doug Quaid
My Beignet Buddy

MT

To Jennifer,
Miss Sunshine

JL

BAD DAY AT MONSTER ELEMENTARY is an original publication of Avon Books. This work has never before appeared in book form.

AVON BOOKS
A division of
The Hearst Corporation
1350 Avenue of the Americas
New York, New York 10019

Copyright © 1995 by Mike Thaler
Illustrations copyright © 1995 by Jared D. Lee Studio, Inc.
Published by arrangement with the author
Library of Congress Catalog Card Number: 94-90718
ISBN: 0-380-77870-X
RL: 2.3

First Avon Camelot Printing: October 1995

CAMELOT TRADEMARK REG. U.S. PAT. OFF. AND IN OTHER COUNTRIES, MARCA REGISTRADA, HECHO EN U.S.A.

Printed in the U.S.A.

QP 10 9 8 7 6 5 4 3 2 1

Mummy Lou had already been to the nurse four times for Band-Aids.

Drac Jr. was hanging upside down in his locker and wouldn't come out.

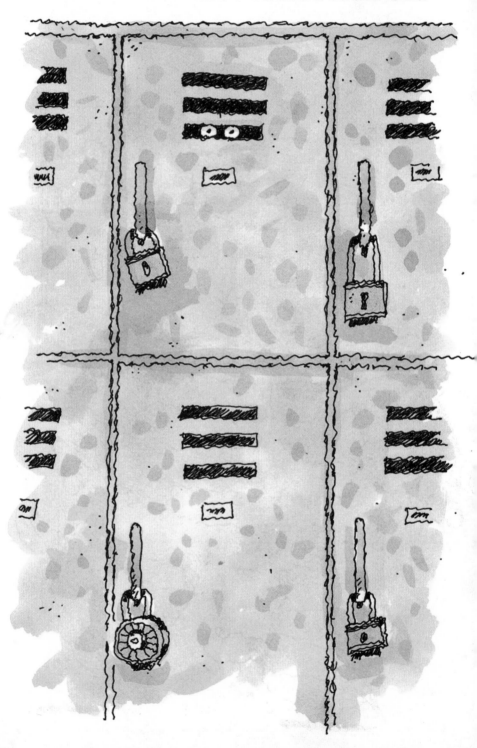

Wolfy was changing in the gym,

and Thing threw up in the hall.

Mr. Potts looked at his desk calendar.
It was **FRIDAY THE 13TH!**
He started to say the Pledge of Allegiance
over the loudspeaker,

when Little Kong
grabbed the cafeteria lady
and climbed the flagpole.

Dr. Frankenstein came in to complain that Franky was failing anatomy.

**Creature from the Black Lagoon
flushed himself down the toilet,**

**and Little Witch was flying
around the halls
on the custodian's broom.**

**Mr. Potts knocked on Drac Jr.'s locker.
All he heard was snoring.**

**Luckily it was recess.
Mr. Potts looked out the window.**

Blobby was hogging the slide again,

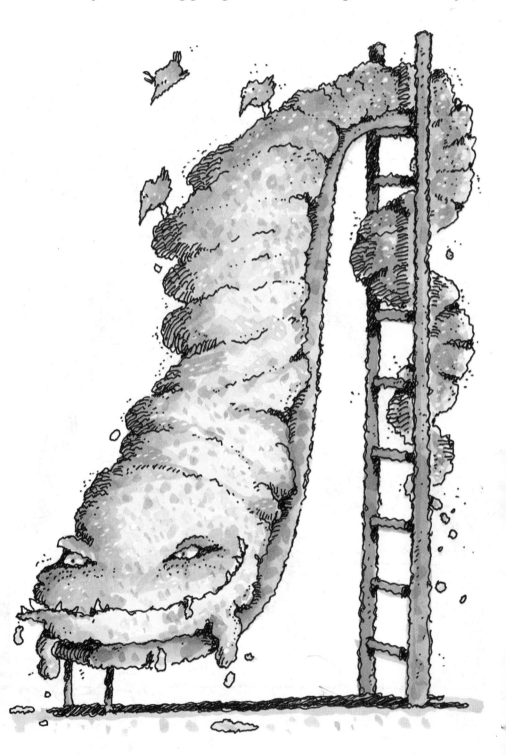

Mummy Lou had buried herself in the sandbox,

Zilla was playing hopscotch...

on the roof,

Franky was playing squash,

and Little Kong was on top of the jungle gym...

with the cafeteria lady.

Then everyone got together
for the class photo.

But Mummy Lou wouldn't smile,

Wolfy wouldn't comb his face,

Blobby was giving everyone rabbit ears,

and no one could find the Invisible Boy.

Lunch wasn't any better.
Franky plugged into the electric socket,

Blobby juggled the custard,

Zilla ate the silverware,

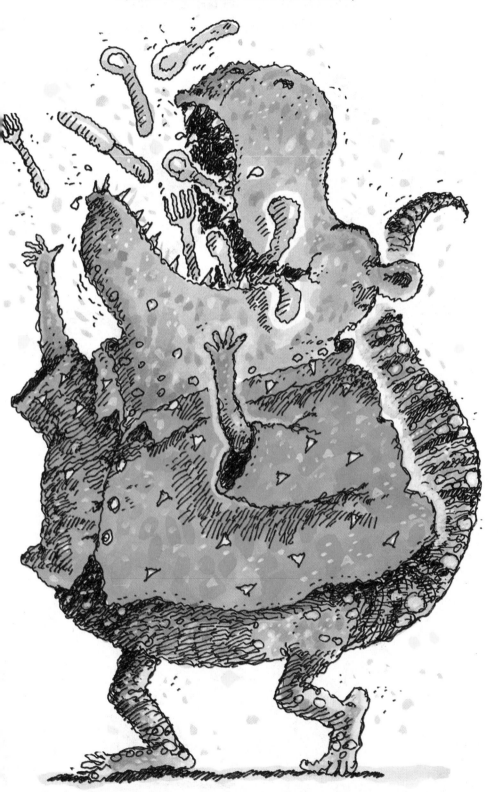

and Drac Jr. drank from the cafeteria lady's neck.

It was going to be a rough afternoon.

Blobby divided in math class

and fingerpainted in art.

Wolfy howled in choir,

Little Kong banged the drum in band,

and Little Witch turned her teacher into a frog during spelling.

Mr. Potts was glad when the bell rang ending the schoolday.

**He waved
as everyone piled onto the buses,
and smiled as they pulled away.**

He whistled all the way back to his office,
put his arms behind his head,
and leaned back in his chair.
Then he froze in horror—
as he looked out the window.
He had forgotten that tonight was...

PARENTS' NIGHT!